Lulu
and the Dog from the Sea

Look out for more books by
Hilary McKay

Lulu and the Duck in the Park

Charlie and the Cat Flap

Charlie and the Great Escape

Charlie and the Big Snow

Charlie and the Rocket Boy

Charlie and the Cheese and Onion Crisps

Charlie and the Haunted Tent

Charlie and the Tooth Fairy

Charlie and the Big Birthday Bash

www.hilarymckay.co.uk

Lulu
and the Dog from the Sea

Hilary McKay

Illustrated by Priscilla Lamont

SCHOLASTIC

For Lissy, with love from
Nanny Kath and Hilary McKay

First published in the UK in 2011 by Scholastic Children's Books
An imprint of Scholastic Ltd
Euston House, 24 Eversholt Street
London, NW1 1DB, UK
Registered office: Westfield Road, Southam, Warwickshire, CV47 0RA
SCHOLASTIC and associated logos are trademarks
and/or registered trademarks of Scholastic Inc.

Text copyright © Hilary McKay, 2011
Illustrations copyright © Priscilla Lamont, 2011

The right of Hilary McKay and Priscilla Lamont to be identified as the
author and illustrator of this work has been asserted by them.

Cover illustration © Priscilla Lamont, 2011

ISBN 978 1 407 11792 8

A CIP catalogue record for this book
is available from the British Library.

Typeset by M Rules
Printed by CPI Bookmarque, Croydon, CR0 4TD

Papers used by Scholastic Children's Books are made
from wood grown in sustainable forests.

1 3 5 7 9 10 8 6 4 2

www.scholastic.co.uk/zone

Chapter One

The Cottage by the Sea

Lulu and Mellie were seven years old. They were cousins and they were friends. Their houses were so close that it took less than five minutes to run between the two. They could visit each other easily without getting lost or squashed on the road.

That was a good thing, because Lulu and Mellie were not just ordinary friends – they were best friends.

They were such good friends they hardly ever quarrelled, although sometimes they did grumble at each other a bit. They mostly grumbled about each other's hobbies, which were not at all alike.

"Colouring in again?" Lulu would say when she went to see why Mellie had forgotten to come and play. "You're *always* colouring in!"

"Cleaning out again?" Mellie would ask, when she came to find out what Lulu had been doing all day. "You're *always* cleaning out!" she would say, holding her nose.

It wasn't true that Mellie was always colouring in. Often she was painting or drawing or making things with glue and glitter and chopped-up paper and lots of mess. But it was true that very often Lulu was cleaning out.

Lulu loved animals and she had a lot of pets.

The rule about pets in Lulu's house was:

The More the Merrier!
As Long as Lulu Cleans Them Out!

Lulu had two guinea pigs, four rabbits, one parrot, one hamster, quite a lot of goldfish and a rather old dog named Sam.

It took a lot of work to look after all these pets. Mostly Lulu did it, but sometimes other people helped her out.

Whenever Lulu's family went on holiday, Mellie's parents would always help. They would do a swop — Lulu's family would take Mellie on holiday, and Mellie's family would take care of Lulu's pets.

All except for Sam the dog, who was going on holiday too. They were all going to stay in a cottage by the sea.

Sam did not think much of that. He didn't enjoy the seaside. He wasn't fond of sand, he didn't like chilly breezes and he hated getting wet in cold salty water. Sam was a small golden teddy-bear-shaped dog. He had short teddy bear legs, and a round teddy bear tummy, and a sweet, stubborn, sleepy teddy bear face.

When Sam went on holiday he took a

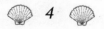

lot of luggage, all packed for him by Lulu.
He took his red blanket and his water bowl
and his food dish and his special biscuits.
Also his dog lead and his dog towels, in
case he got wet, and his shampoo and his
brushes, in case he got sticky.

Sam also took his basket and his red
velvety beanbag.

Sam loved his beanbag very much

 5

and if he did not have it in his basket
he could not go to sleep. Nobody else
could go to sleep either, because Sam
walked around howling and whining and
moaning. It was very important not to
forget the beanbag. Lulu's father checked
a dozen times that it was safely in the
car. He did not want to have to drive all
the way home for it in the middle of the
night, as he had once had to do.

Sam's luggage took up so much space
that it was a good thing Lulu and Mellie
had brought as little as possible. Their
only big thing was Mellie's Build Your
Own Kite Kit. Mellie had been given this
for a birthday present. She had opened it
to admire the strings and the special kite
paper, the bright pens and the exciting
instructions. But then she had put it away
again to save for this seaside holiday.

Now the kite kit was on the back seat. All the things that would not fit anywhere else were there too, piled around Lulu and Mellie.

"It's part of the holiday feeling," said Mellie. "Being all squashed up, hardly able to breathe."

"It's fair that Sam should have the most space," agreed Lulu, "because really he'd rather not come on holiday at all. He'd rather be comfortable."

"This might be a comfortable holiday!" said Lulu's mother hopefully. That made everyone hoot with laughter. They spent the first part of the journey reminding one another about holidays in the past.

"Like the time we went to Scotland and left behind the bag that had everyone's shoes," said Lulu.

"Or that house we stayed in that had a

ghost in the attic," said Mellie.

"Or that place where the chimney was struck by lightning and fell down into the living room," said Lulu's father.

Lulu's mother groaned and said perhaps they should turn back and not go away after all.

"They were lovely holidays," said Lulu and Mellie, who had enjoyed the lightning and the ghost and the new shoes very much.

They were very much looking forward to staying in a little seaside town.

That was what they thought, but the first thing they discovered about the cottage was that it was not near the town at all. It was all on its own, down a bumpy, potholed track. Bumps made Sam sick. So Lulu's father drove very slowly indeed, trying to dodge the biggest holes, while Lulu's mother twisted round, watching for the gulps that meant Sam had to be flung out of the car as quickly as possible. Meanwhile, Mellie was ignoring both Sam and the bumpy road and saying, "Should I unpack my kite now, now we're nearly there? I think I could just open it and get out the bits. . ."

"No!" said Lulu's mother and father, but they said it too late. Mellie was already unpacking. When car fell into another hole, important-looking pieces of kite spilled everywhere, and Mellie began to moan.

"Just what I didn't want to happen!" she grumbled, turning herself upside down to try and gather the pieces from the floor.

"Call this a road?" complained Lulu's

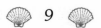 9

father. "It's just one giant crater after
another!"

"Now the string's come unwound!"
cried Mellie.

Sam made a noise like a sort of cough.

"Nearly there, Sam!" said Lulu's mother
hopefully, winding down her window.

Only Lulu sat quietly, gazing at the
view. Ahead, she saw a white cottage and
green grass. Every few minutes, she saw
glimpses of a sea that gleamed dark grey
or silver bright.

All along the edge of the sea Lulu could see a mountain range of sand dunes. Strange bushes grew on them with dim grey leaves and orange berries. Strange ribbon-like blue-green grasses were combed by the sea wind. Strange narrow sandy paths twisted and climbed and suddenly vanished.

And all among the bushes and grass and sandy paths a strange animal leapt and ran, watching the car. It moved so quickly that the only thing Lulu could see clearly was its strange, flapping ears.

They were ears like brown paper bags.

The owner of the cottage was waiting for them when they arrived. Everyone except Mellie (who was still scrabbling up pieces of kite) tumbled out of the car, all stiff and achey with travelling.

"Took your time, didn't you?" said the cottage owner as Lulu's parents smiled and called "Hello!". "I saw you, dithering along that track, like there was all the time in the world!"

"Well!" began Lulu's father. "It's quite a obstacle course, that track. . ."

"You've got the wrong sort of car!" said the cottage owner. "You need something much bigger! Hurry up! Come inside and I'll give you the key. Shoes off!" she added sternly.

"It's very kind of you to have waited,"

said Lulu's mother, as she and Lulu's father followed her to the door.

"Had to," snapped the cottage owner, grimly. "I needed to warn you about that dog!"

"Sam?" asked Lulu, but the cottage owner had disappeared, with Lulu's parents after her.

Bang! went the door, in a most unfriendly way.

"Why's she so . . ." began Mellie, staring.

"Shush!" warned Lulu.

". . . cross?" finished Mellie loudly,

dropping bits of kite all over the ground as she spoke. "Don't worry! She can't hear! She's shut the door. Why do you think she said that about Sam?"

Lulu couldn't imagine. Sam was behaving perfectly. He had survived the bumps without being sick, and now he was doing what he always did at the end of a car journey: unpacking his biscuit bowl.

On days when Sam was going in the car he was only ever given a very small breakfast. Now he wanted the rest of it. He stood up on his teddy bear legs, dragged his bowl from amongst his mountain of luggage, carried it in his teeth to Lulu and dropped it at her feet.

It was Lulu's job to fill it up as quickly as possible.

As usual, she rushed to do it, and as

usual Sam stood and watched, stumpy tail wagging, with a smile on his teddy bear face.

From inside the cottage Lulu's parents could see all this happening. Lulu's mother asked worriedly, "Why do you want to warn us about our dog? We did tell you we were bringing him."

"Your dog?" asked the cottage owner, looking out of the window at the happy sight of Sam gobbling biscuits. "I wasn't talking about your dog! He's a poor old thing, isn't he? Looks more like a sheep. . . *That* dog!"

She jabbed a pointing finger in the direction of the sand dunes, where a small sandstorm had just erupted.

The sandstorm rolled down the sand dunes, arrived between Lulu and Mellie in a cloud of dust, seized the packet of

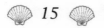

dog biscuits that Lulu had only a moment
before put down, whirled round and
raced away, all in one astonishing moment.

"*WAR! WAR! WAR!*" barked Sam,
nearly falling over with rage.

"*That* dog!" said the cottage owner,
rushing out of the cottage with Lulu's
parents behind her. "That dog!" she
repeated, pointing to a dusty blur on the
sand dunes. "That dog from the sea! He's
a thief! He's a menace! The people last

week lost a whole roasted chicken from under their noses! Nothing is safe from him and no one can get near him. We've had the dogcatcher out twice already and he's never got close enough to grab—"

"Oh, poor dog!" exclaimed Lulu.

"Don't you go encouraging him," said the woman, turning on her quite fiercely. "He's not welcome round here! You'll have to be careful. No leaving out picnics, nor scraps for the seagulls. He goes all through the rubbish too. So you'll have to remember to take the dustbin into the house at night!"

"*Take the dustbin into the house at night?*" repeated Lulu's father, staring.

"I've warned you and now I must be off," said the cottage owner.

"Did you say, 'Take. . .'?"

"I did," said the cottage owner,

 *17*

dragging a bike from the hedge. Then she handed Lulu's mother a large and rather rusty key, and rode off.

"TAKE THE DUSTBIN INTO THE HOUSE AT NIGHT!" exploded Lulu's father wildly, the moment she was gone. "What kind of place is it where you have to do that?"

Lulu and Mellie became helpless with giggles and rolled about on the grass.

"And you're not helping!" complained Lulu's father as he stepped over them.

"Oh!" said Mellie. "I love this place!"

"You haven't seen inside yet," warned Lulu's mother. "And neither have we, hardly! I thought she might stay and show us where things are . . . and explain about hot water, and how the cooker works. . . Oh well, never mind! Who's coming with me to explore?"

Lulu and Mellie scrambled to their feet, and hurried to follow her into the cottage.

It was very clean.

And very bare.

It was just four little rooms: two bedrooms, a kitchen and a living room, with a very damp-smelling bathroom tacked on to the back. The water in the taps was as cold as ice, and the cooker (said a neat label that was stuck on the front) was waiting for a part for its oven.

"No wonder Mrs-on-the-Bike hopped

it so fast!" said Lulu's father, and he went outside and looked suspiciously at the chimney to see if it had been struck by lightning. It looked quite solid, however, and there was no ghost in the attic because there was no attic. There was no upstairs at all.

"Well, at least we all have shoes this time!" said Lulu's father, cheering up. "So maybe we'll survive!"

Lulu and Mellie were sure they would. Their bedroom window faced the sand dunes. They pushed it open and the sea wind blew in, and there they were, nearly amongst the blue-green grasses and grey, orange-berried bushes. Almost next to the little gold paths down which a dog from the sea might swoop like a storm.

"It's the most perfect place ever," said Lulu.

 20

Her mother said "Hmmm" to that. She was exploring the kitchen cupboards. She had just discovered that there were not enough mugs for all four of them to have hot drinks at once, and not enough glasses for all four of them to have cold drinks at once either. And she discovered other things about saucepans and forks and spoons that made her say "Hmmm" as well.

"But we *do* have shoes," said Lulu's father. "So let's go and explore!"

So they did.

Chapter Two

The Dog From the Sea

"I should like to know much, much more about the dog from the sea," said Lulu.

There was no sign of him in the sand dunes, nor on the wide windy beach. No dog with paper-bag ears splashed in the pools by the breakwaters, or raced across the golf course (where no dogs were allowed). But as they got nearer to the town end of the beach they heard news.

The ice cream and hot dog stall knew

him very well. They had lost more than one sausage to his thieving ways.

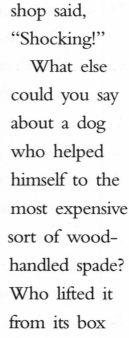

The lady from the bucket and spade shop said, "Shocking!"

What else could you say about a dog who helped himself to the most expensive sort of wood-handled spade? Who lifted it from its box by the postcard stand, galloped off with it clamped in his jaws, chewed it to shreds, left the bits on the sand and came back, tail wagging, for another!

"But where did he come from?" asked Lulu.

"He came from the back of The Golden Lotus," said the lady from the bucket and spade shop.

The Golden Lotus was a Chinese restaurant. There was a whole street of little restaurants in the town. Indian and Chinese and Italian and Thai and a fish and chip shop at the end. And behind the shops was a small messy space, full of crates and boxes, rubbish bins and bottle banks and other things like old fridges waiting to be taken away.

It was a great untidy muddle, the shop lady told Lulu, and in the most untidy bit of the muddle, under a pile of crates and cardboard boxes behind The Golden Lotus, the mother of the dog from the sea had made a den.

Three puppies had been born in that den: the dog from the sea, and the dog from the sea's two sisters.

All through the spring they lived together, a wild and happy life. In the daytime they slept, all flung in a warm heap under the crates.

At night they went hunting with their mother. She was a very clever dog, and she knew all the places to find things to eat. Seaside towns with hungry visitors have lots of spare food, either thrown into

bins or dropped
on the streets. The
mother dog taught
her three puppies
how to crawl under
the fence near

the fairground and how to climb into
a rubbish skip. She showed them how
to push over a bin, and how to chase
a seagull from a handful of chips. She
showed her wild family every single thing
it was possible for a dog to eat.

What good dogs, thought Lulu as
she listened. What a
lot of cleaning
up they had
done. People
should have
been very
grateful, she thought.

But people were not grateful. Not even at The Golden Lotus, where the dogs cleared up most of all.

They sent for the dogcatcher.

Two dogcatchers came. A very tall man, and a very tall woman. They spoke to the dogs with kind voices.

First they caught the two sisters. They put them in two cages, where they howled and cried so loudly their mother came to rescue them.

That made it easy for the dogcatchers to catch her as well.

Very soon there were three dogs in three cages.

The last of the wild dog family watched in horror. He did not know what happened to a dog after it was caught in a cage. He had never heard of vets, or rescue homes, or the friendly people who visit them and say *"That's the dog for me!"*. All he knew was what he saw and heard: his sisters crying, his mother frantic, tearing at the cage.

He watched, but he watched from a distance. He guessed they had a cage for him too, and he was right – they did.

But they could not get him in to it.

When the dogcatchers turned to the last wild dog, and spoke in their kind voices, the wild dog ran for his life.

He ran to the sand dunes, and there he hid.

That was how the wild dog became the dog from the sea.

For a long time he would sneak back to the crate pile behind The Golden Lotus, just in case the dogcatchers had changed their minds and allowed his family to come back. But at last he gave up hope.

He lived among the sand dunes, a wild hungry life. He stole all he could, and he ate whatever he could swallow, and sometimes it made him ill and sometimes it made him stronger. He got used to that. He got used to the long thirsty waits to drink from the stream that crossed the golf course or from the paddling pool near the town. He got used to cold winds and the thorns on the grey bushes, but he never got used to being alone.

The dog from the sea was terribly lonely.

As the weather grew warmer, more and

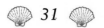

more people came to the beach. Grown-up people and children. The dog from the sea kept away from the grown-ups in case they had cages, but he watched the children. He was tremendously interested in the games they played, and the holes they dug and the balls they threw. He watched from the sand dunes, wagging his tail, bouncing with excitement when they yelled at the waves, dribbling as they ate their picnics.

When the beach emptied at night-time he inspected the places where they had been. Sometimes he found a lost toy. These he carried away as if they were great treasures. The sand dunes were dotted with shoes and burst balls and other things he had found.

The dogcatchers did not forget the dog from the sea. Every now and then they would return and try to catch him. They never could. The dog was too good at hiding and the sand dunes were too huge. The little sandy paths wound through them like paths in a maze.

The dog from the sea knew them all. Every tangled track in the grass. Every tunnel beneath the bushes. Every secret sandy hollow. Every lookout place.

One of the lookout places was right above the little white cottage. The dog from the sea liked the cottage. Roasted chickens lived in the kitchen there, and whole boxes of dog biscuits lay unguarded on the grass.

There was a dustbin like a treasure chest too. Sometimes it vanished at night, but sometimes it didn't. It depended who was staying in the cottage.

On Saturday night, last thing before

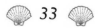 33

Lulu's father went to bed, he stepped outside and breathed a deep breath. There was a lovely smell of sea air and short green grass. There was an unlovely smell of something else.

"I'm *not!*" said Lulu's father. "I'm *just* not! I'm just not taking that *dustbin* into the house at night!"

Chapter Three

Sunday

When Lulu and Mellie woke up on Sunday morning, there, right outside the window, was Lulu's father. He had a bin bag and a pointy stick and Lulu's seaside spade for scooping. There was rubbish all over the garden – not just the little bit of rubbish that Lulu's family had thrown away, but also everything left behind from the people who had stayed in the cottage the week before.

"The dog from the sea must have been

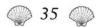

to visit!" said Lulu, and she was pleased.

"He's made a terrible mess," said Mellie.

"Perhaps we will have to take the bin into the house at night after all," said Lulu's mother at breakfast time, but she wrinkled her nose as she spoke.

"Certainly not!" said Lulu's father. "I've thought of what to do. I shall get some big rocks from the beach and use them as weights on the lid of the bin."

"You're not supposed to do that!" said Lulu. "There's a notice on the beach that says NO STONES OR ROCKS TO BE TAKEN AWAY."

"I won't take them away," said Lulu's father. "I'll just borrow them for a little while."

"Will you put them back?" asked Mellie.

"Of course."

"Carry them right across the sand dunes back to the beach?"

"Absolutely."

"And put them exactly where you found them? How will you remember?"

"I'll draw a map."

"What if someone sees you?" said Lulu. "Even if you draw a map and even if you take them back and even if they're only borrowed, you'll still look like a rock burglar!"

For a moment Lulu's father looked rather sad. He didn't want to look like a rock burglar. Then he had a good idea.

"I shall smuggle them! Under my jumper or hidden in a bag! I'll locate the rocks, draw a map, mark their positions, borrow them (*borrow*, not take!) and then I'll smuggle them across the sand dunes! And use them on the dustbin lid!"

Lulu's father looked very happy at this thought. He was pleased to have an excuse to do some smuggling on his seaside holiday.

"It will be good for my fitness training," he said. "I've decided to run the next London marathon! This holiday I am going to do press-ups and weights and a lot of running. Anyone who likes can come with me!"

"This holiday I am going to read and read," said Lulu's mother. "I never get time to read at home. I've brought six books, one for each day, and *War and Peace* for a spare! Anyone who likes can borrow the ones I'm not reading!"

"This holiday I'm going to make my kite *perfectly*," said Mellie. "Every bit perfect, like the picture on the box. Anyone who likes can help me!"

"This holiday," said Lulu, "I'm going to find the dog from the sea, make friends with him, tame him so that he doesn't run away and—"

That was as much as Lulu managed to say before everyone started talking at once, saying what a bad idea they thought it was, and how it could never happen,

and even if it did, what then? It wouldn't
be kind to the dog from the sea to make
friends with him and tame him. He
would have to be left behind at the end
of the week, anyway.

"Why?" asked Lulu.
"What about the more
the merrier, as long
as I clean them out?"

"That's hamsters
and goldfish and rabbits
and things!" her mother told
her. "Not dogs! Think of
Sam!"

"Sam would hate it,"
said Lulu's father. "He's
an only dog sort of dog."

That was true.

Sam could put up with parrots and
he quite liked goldfish. He didn't mind

guinea pigs. He was only slightly annoyed by hamsters and rabbits.

But dogs he could not bear!

Sam thought dogs were smelly and noisy and greedy. They were his least favourite animals, even worse than cats.

Sam didn't know, and would never have guessed, that he was a dog himself.

"But who will look after the dog from the sea?" asked Lulu.

"Someone," said her mother.

"Not us," said her father, and then both of them said, "Not sensible! Not going to

happen! Not even slightly possible!"

Lulu did not argue. She had found that arguing only made people argue back. It was better, she thought, to do exactly as you liked, quietly, with no fuss. Besides, what did her mad family know about possible and impossible?

As if it were even slightly possible that her father would ever run a marathon!

Or that her mother would read six books in six days ending with *War and Peace* (which she had been trying to read ever since before Lulu was born).

Or even that Mellie would perfectly finish her kite, which was already spread all over the living room floor with the string in knots and the instructions missing.

"Never mind," said Mellie. "I never bother with boring instructions anyway."

"How can you make it without

instructions?" wondered Lulu.

"I'll just copy the picture on the box."

"It'll take ages."

"Not if you help," said Mellie, looking around to check Lulu's parents were out of the way, and adding, "You help me with my kite and I'll help you with the dog from the sea."

Lulu thought how much she liked Mellie, who never thought anything was impossible.

"I'll help you as soon as we come back from the beach," she promised.

The way to the beach was straight out of the door and over the sand dunes.

A path of soft,
sliding sand
climbed up and
down.

A leg-aching sort of path.

"We should have brought camels," said
Lulu's father as they slipped and dropped
things and tumbled over Sam,

who kept
stopping for
rests where people were
about to tread.

Lulu was looking out for the dog
from the sea. She had filled her pockets
with dog biscuits before she left the
cottage. Now she lagged behind the others
and scattered them along the path as
she walked.

Just in case, thought Lulu.

Not many people came to their end of the beach. Most of the other families on holiday were far away. The windbreakers and picnic rugs where they had set up their camps looked like tiny bright patches in the distance.

Lulu's family made a camp too, a very large one, because there seemed to be so many things they could not do without.

Books and spades and training weights, the frisbee and the towels. The picnic rug and picnic things. The windbreaker because Sam did not like chilly breezes. Sam's beanbag, so that he could snooze in comfort, and, of course, his biscuit dish and his water bowl and a big bottle of water.

The dog from the sea found his trail of biscuits very quickly, and after that it did not take him long to find Lulu and the camp. From high up on the sand dunes he watched everything that happened. The longer he watched, the more interested he became.

Some of the things he saw were very puzzling. Lulu's mother, for instance, reading her book, turning the pages, not looking up, saying, "Hmmm, hmmm," when anyone spoke to her. *A strange way to behave*, thought the dog from the sea.

Lulu and Mellie were not so mysterious. They were chasing a round toy that flew through the air. As soon as they caught it they flung it away. They made happy noises unless they fell over. Then they squealed. If they squealed very loudly the person with the book said, "Hmmm?"

But she still didn't look up.

Lulu's father was not mysterious at all. He was collecting things, just like the dog did himself sometimes. Safe at a distance, the dog watched him toil through the sand dunes – backwards and forwards, smuggling rocks.

Then there was Sam.

The dog from the sea had been so busy looking at the people that he did not notice Sam until Lulu's mother put down her book and called, "What about our picnic?"

Then he noticed him.

Sam ate biscuits and pizza and jam tarts and brown bread and cream cheese sandwiches, and the dog from the sea watched every bite. He wanted the sandwiches so much he cried a little as he saw them vanish, but the thing he longed for most of all was Sam's water bowl.

The beach was a thirsty place for a dog to live. The golf course stream at one end was guarded by golfers. The paddling pool at the other end was guarded by paddlers.

When the dog from the sea saw Sam's water bowl brimming with clear water he crept closer and closer.

The food was all gone. The last of the pizza and jam tarts and brown bread and cream cheese all eaten up.

Lulu's mother put down her book, stretched her arms, and wandered off to collect shells.

Lulu's father did some stretches and set off to jog along the surf.

Only Lulu and Mellie and Sam were left.

The dog from the sea was hardly frightened at all of people who were Lulu and Mellie's size. And he had a strong feeling that he could run faster than Sam.

And he was very thirsty. He took a step forward, and then another, creeping

through the sand-dune grasses . . . then
suddenly Sam saw him.

"*WAR! WAR! WAR!*" barked Sam.

"*WAR! WAR! WAR!*" and he tumbled
off his beanbag.

"*WAR! WAR! WAR!*" and he actually
set off at a teddy bear trot towards the
dog from the sea.

The dog from the sea sank lower and
lower into the blue-green grasses as Sam
came near.

He sank until
he was invisible.

Then he gave
a great leap and
jumped right
over Sam.

He landed
in front of the
water bowl.

There was a sound like a drain, and the bowl was empty — slurped dry in one enormous slurp by the dog from the sea.

"*WAR!*" roared Sam.

The dog from the sea ran, trampling his great sandy paws over Sam's beanbag on the way.

"*WAR!*" howled Sam furiously, and he would have gone after him if Lulu had not grabbed his collar.

"Shush!" she told Sam, while Mellie refilled his water bowl, and to the dog from the sea Lulu called, "Good dog! It's all right! Good dog!"

High on the sand dunes the dog heard, and was happy.

He had never been called a good dog before.

He liked it.

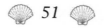 *51*

Lulu and Millie did not see the dog from the sea again that day. In the afternoon they walked into the town to bounce on the giant trampolines. That was fun. Afterwards they went back to the cottage to start work on Mellie's kite.

Even with all the family's help that was not easy at all.

Includes Everything Needed To Build This Magnificent Kite!

read the writing on the box.

Lulu's father said there had been a printing error. He said it should read *Nothing* instead of *Everything*.

The bare little cottage was not much help. It didn't contain any useful kite-making things. Just before the shops closed they sent Lulu's father out in the car to buy scissors and glue and something sharp that would drill tiny holes.

"And while you are shopping you might get a couple of new mugs," said Lulu's mother. "And some bread and some salad and some sausages, and a tin opener that works. And a tea towel or two would be useful. . ."

Lulu's father groaned. Shopping was his least favourite thing to do, and driving through potholes was his second least favourite. He drove away before they could think of any more things they needed.

"Sticky tape," remembered Mellie,

watching the dust fly up as he bumped down the track.

"More dog biscuits and a frying pan," added Lulu's mother. "Oh well, we'll send him again tomorrow! Poor thing! Never mind. We'll be extra kind to him when he comes back."

They were very kind to Lulu's father when he came bumping home. They let him barbecue the sausages, and afterwards they played rounders with him and then they helped him pile his smuggled rocks on to the dustbin lid, and then they all went to bed.

Everyone went to sleep at once.

Except Lulu.

Lulu thought about the dog from the sea.

She thought about the smuggled rocks piled up on the bin.

And she thought how painful it would be

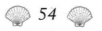 54

if those rocks were to fall on anyone's nose.

As soon as Lulu had thought these thoughts she climbed out of bed.

And then out of the window.

Then she went to the bin and began lifting the rocks from its lid. She had to concentrate hard while she was doing this, because of the danger of dropping them on her bare feet. She did not look up until she had lifted down the last rock, and then she nearly jumped out of her skin.

The dog from the sea was creeping towards her like a hungry wolf.

("I think I would have screamed," said Mellie, when Lulu told her the next day.)

Lulu managed not to scream. Instead she said, as she had said before, "Good dog! It's all right! Good dog!"

The dog's tail began to swing with pleasure.

 55

"Good dog," said Lulu encouragingly, and she lifted the lid from the bin and fished out a burnt sausage.

The dog ate all the burnt sausages, and he drank two buckets full of water (collected for him by Lulu by way of the bedroom window). Then he and Lulu sat down together, and Lulu stroked him, being careful not to touch the itchy patches where his fleas had made him scratch away his fur. Often she said "Good dog" as she stroked, and every time she said it the dog's tail beat with happiness.

That was how Lulu and the dog from the sea made friends.

Chapter Four

Monday and Tuesday

On Monday Lulu's family spent the day exploring the local castle. It had cannons round the walls and a telescope on top of the battlements. With the telescope you could look right over the sand dunes. Lulu looked for a long time, while a fidgety queue built up behind her, but she did not see the dog from the sea.

A chilly wind blew over the battlements, straight through their fleeces and cold on their skin.

"Let's go home and make my kite," said Mellie.

On the box of Mellie's kite, under:

Includes Everything Needed To Build This Magnificent Kite!

It also said:

Not suitable for children under the age of 36 months.

Underneath this Lulu's father had written:

Or anyone living down a potholey track.

The kite in the kit was plain white plastic. That was so that you could draw your own picture. This was the part that Mellie had looked forward to most. She planned to cover the white plastic with rainbow-coloured seagulls.

It was a very big kite. It would take a lot of rainbow seagulls to cover the whole surface.

"Anyone who likes can draw seagulls on my kite," said Mellie, tipping out felt pens all over the floor.

The problem was, anyone couldn't.

The pens were all dried up. One after another Mellie pulled off their lids, discovered their ghostly shadows, and flung them away.

"It's not fair!" she wailed.

Lulu did not think it was fair either. "Brand new pens all dried up!" she exclaimed indignantly.

"I hadn't used them once!" said Mellie sadly. "Well, once, maybe. . . Or a few times. . . I'll never get this kite made. I might as well stop trying."

Bump, bump, bump went the car through the potholes on an emergency expedition to save Mellie from despair. They bought new pens and candyfloss and a mountain of chips with curry sauce. The candyfloss got in their hair and the curry sauce smelled much nicer than it tasted, but by bedtime a flock of seagulls as bright as flowers blossomed across the kite.

And that was another day over.

The dog from the sea did not come creeping like a wolf that night. He came trotting down the garden path like a friend on a visit. He was very pleased indeed with his chips and curry sauce. He swallowed in big hungry gulps and drank a bucketful of water.

As he drank, Lulu noticed his paper-bag ears. They were all tangled round with bramble stems. The brambles were so knotted into his fur that Lulu could not pull them free.

"I'll have to fetch the kite scissors," she whispered to the dog. She was most surprised a minute later to hear a voice call, "Here!"

"Mellie!"

"I've been watching," said Mellie,

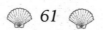

passing the scissors out of the window.
"Careful you don't make him too tame,
Lulu!"

"Why?" asked Lulu, beginning to snip.

"Oh," said Mellie, slowly. "Because it
might not be safe to be too tame . . ."

The bramble strands pulled loose. The
dog shook his paper-bag ears back into
their proper places.

". . . if he doesn't want to be caught," said Mellie.

Until that moment the dog had not noticed Mellie.

Suddenly, now he did. Perhaps because the snipping had stopped. Maybe because his ears were free at last. Whatever the reason, the dog from the sea gave Mellie a swift glance. Sudden alarm seemed to show in his eyes. His body went still.

"Good dog! It's all right," Lulu told him. "Good dog!"

The alarm seemed to fade. Very slowly the dog's tail began swinging again.

"He trusts you," said Mellie.

He did, but he was still nervous. At the sudden rustle of a chip paper he backed away. A moment later, when Lulu accidentally rattled the dustbin lid, he vanished completely.

"He'll be back again tomorrow," said Lulu.

Tuesday was a day of grey skies and sudden showers.

"There's a cliff-top walk we really should try," said Lulu's father, getting out his map.

Sam knew about maps and very long walks and he went and hid behind the sofa.

"I know how he feels," said Lulu's mother, but she did not hide behind the sofa. She built a driftwood fire and settled down in front of it with her third holiday book.

Behind the sofa Sam found Mellie's kite box. A long smooth stick fell out when he pushed it. Sam chewed it to pieces.

The silvery driftwood burnt with pale-blue flames, and the room became warm. Lulu and Mellie and Lulu's father bumped away in the car. Sam thought it might be safe to come out from behind the sofa. He settled down in front of the fire with a second long stick from the box . . .

"My kite struts!" shrieked Mellie, the moment she walked through the door.

When she had calmed down a bit, Lulu's father explained that nothing in the world was easier to make than kite struts.

And that he would do it, in a moment. Beautifully and perfectly. Better than the originals. Out of any old straight bit of washed-up driftwood they could find.

After that the whole family hunted for washed-up driftwood in straight enough pieces to make new struts for a kite. They hunted until it was too dark to see, but they didn't find any.

And then they went sadly back to the cottage and ate omelettes and chocolate cake to cheer themselves up. It was a rather dismal evening, despite the chocolate cake and the loveliness of the driftwood fire. Mellie put all her bits of kite on the table, the seagull picture and the chewed wood and the tangled strings and the plastic loops for threading who-knew-what through (since the instructions had been lost) and she said to Lulu, "You said you'd help."

"I will help," said Lulu.

"Well, think of something!"

An idea came to Lulu like a present from the sky. She told her mother and her mother gave her a great happy hug. She told her father, and he said she was a genius. She would have told Mellie, but Mellie covered her ears and said, "Don't tell me, don't tell me, in case it doesn't work."

That night, the dog from the sea was waiting for Lulu. He ate omelette and toast and chocolate cake, a lot of dog biscuits and a large piece of cheese. More thorns and tangles were snipped from his fur. Once again, Mellie watched from the window, but this time he was much less nervous.

"I think he might like me after all," whispered Mellie.

"Of course he does," said Lulu.

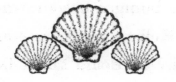

Chapter Five

Wednesday and Thursday

They woke up on Wednesday to a day of bright sunshine.

"I am going shopping; I may be some time," said Lulu's mother, climbing into the car.

"What sort of shopping?" asked Mellie.

"Secret shopping," said Lulu's mother, and to Lulu she whispered, "Operation Kite!"

Then she bumped away down the dusty track with Sam to keep her company.

Lulu and Mellie and Lulu's father

 69

headed for the beach. It was a much easier journey over the sand dunes without Sam and his beanbag. Lulu's father went swimming, and Lulu and Mellie went paddling. However, no one stayed in long because, as Lulu's father pointed out, the sea was very close to freezing and if it froze over completely they'd be stuck in the ice. Afterwards, Lulu and Mellie went off to play, while Lulu's father did some exercises to get the numbness from his hands and feet.

Lulu and Mellie had not been playing for more than five minutes when a head with paper-bag ears looked over the sand dunes.

The dog from the sea had come to play too.

At first he just played beside them. When Lulu and Mellie raced after the

frisbee, the dog from
the sea raced after an
invisible frisbee
of his own.
When they
peered into rock
pools, he peered

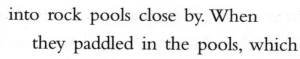

into rock pools close by. When
they paddled in the pools, which
were much warmer
than the sea, the
dog paddled too,
sneezing at the
splashes. And
then they
got out two tubs of bubbles.

The dog from the
sea could not resist
the bubbles. He
raced to catch them,

snapped at them in the air, and looked astonished when they vanished. He loved it when Lulu and Mellie laughed at him. His tail wagged and his paper-bag ears flapped and he bounced like a dog on springs.

When Lulu's mother arrived with Sam and his beanbag, and a thumbs-up sign for Lulu and a hug for Mellie, and a picnic and a handful of dripping ice creams, the dog from the sea did not run away.

He stayed and shared the picnic.

He didn't come very close. He didn't quite trust Lulu's parents not to be secret dogcatchers, but still, he stayed.

If Sam had not been worn out by shopping he would not have let this happen. But shopping had tired Sam completely. He lay down on his beanbag and closed his eyes so that he could not see the dog from the sea, with the frisbee as a plate, eating sausage rolls and cheese sandwiches, and drinking water from Lulu's bucket.

"Now!" said Lulu's mother, when the picnic was all finished. "You'll never guess what I bought this morning, Mellie!"

"What?"

"A build-your-own-kite kit just like the one you had!" said Lulu's mother triumphantly. "So now we have all the pieces, AND new strings with no knots AND the proper instructions!"

"Oh!" gasped Mellie, hugging her. "Was that what you thought of, Lulu, last night?"

"I told you I'd help!" said Lulu proudly, and her father said, "Come on! Back to the cottage, everyone, for Operation Kite!"

Operation Kite took Lulu's parents and Mellie all afternoon, and except for the seagull picture on the front, it was all new kite.

"It's the picture on the front that matters," said Mellie, cheerfully.

Lulu did not help with the kite-making. Instead, she spent the afternoon on the grassy patch outside the house, playing with the dog from the sea.

It was very, very different from playing with Sam. If you threw a ball for Sam to fetch he would try not to look, unless you happened to be someone he loved very much. If you were, he would get slowly to his feet. Slowly, slowly he would walk to the ball, pick it up in his teeth as if it tasted nasty, and then slowly bring it back to you, spit it out, and sigh.

The sigh meant, "Please don't do that again. I shall not fetch it twice."

Very different from the dog from the sea, who hurtled after balls so fast he skidded and rolled in somersaults. Who could catch a frisbee in his teeth. Who understood the game of tag, and played it round and round the little white cottage.

Lulu and the dog from the sea played so hard, they didn't notice the cottage owner coming silently along the track to the cottage.

The cottage owner liked to visit the cottage now and then, to check that her guests were behaving as she thought they should behave.

Just in case they weren't.

Lulu wasn't.

Halfway along the track the cottage owner saw Lulu and the dog from the sea.

She paused.

She got off her bike.

She glared.

She puffed with fury.

Then she turned round, and rode off again, as quickly as she could to telephone the dogcatchers.

The dogcatchers came quickly with a cage, a long stick with a collar on the end, a handful of dog biscuits, and the cottage owner following behind.

Lulu took a little while to understand what was happening. At first she just stood and stared, her hand on the neck of the dog from the sea. Then she saw the van, and the collar on a stick, and the cottage owner, very eager, rushing up with her bike.

Lulu screamed and clutched the dog from the sea.

"That's right, hang on to him!" screeched the cottage owner, while from inside the cottage ran Lulu's parents and

Mellie, and Sam barking "*WAR! WAR! WAR!*"

"Stand still, *please!*" begged one of the two dogcatchers. "Oooofff!"

That was the sound made when Mellie flung herself head first into the nearest dogcatcher's stomach.

"*Mellie!*" exclaimed Lulu's mother, grabbing her.

"*WAR! WAR! WAR!*" roared Sam, at the dogcatchers and the cottage owner, and at the dog from the sea, trembling with fear under Lulu's hand.

"Get that dog!" shouted the wicked witch of a cottage owner. "He's a thief! He's a menace! He wants putting away!"

"NO!" shouted Lulu, and she stopped holding on to the dog from the sea. She pushed him away and cried, "Run!"

★

There had been two friends playing, blue-green grass, and a blue and white sky.

Now there was noise and trouble and anger. And the dog from the sea was gone, running for his life.

 79

That night Lulu waited and waited, but the dog from the sea did not come to visit the cottage.

"Do you think he's thinking of me like I am thinking of him?" she asked Mellie.

"Yes," said Mellie.

Much later in the night Mellie said, "I think you should stop climbing in and out of the window."

"I can't get to sleep."

"No one could get to sleep," said Mellie, "if they kept climbing in and out of a window."

"Why aren't you sad?" demanded Lulu.

"I am sad," said Mellie. "About the poor dog from the sea, I'm sad! About how frightened he was, and how he looked at you to see if it was true, and

how he saw that it was true, and ran,
I'm sad about that! I helped, didn't I?
I charged that dogcatcher as hard as I
could!"

"Yes, you did," admitted Lulu.

"But I am not completely sad because
I can't help feeling happy about my kite.
I thought we'd never fix it, and now we
have, and it's perfect. Don't you think
that's good?"

"You know I do," said Lulu. "It was me
that thought of the way to fix it."

"Tomorrow," said Mellie, "we can fly
my kite on the beach. It will show for
miles and miles. The dog will see it and
come running."

That was a happy thought.

Lulu fell asleep thinking it.

Chapter Six

Thursday and Friday

Early on Thursday morning Mellie woke everyone up, hurried them through breakfast and chased them out of the house.

"What's all this pushing and rushing?" demanded Lulu's father. "It's the last day of the holiday! Shouldn't we make the most of it and have a little peace?"

"It's because it's the last day!" said Mellie.

"What do you want peace for, anyway?" asked Lulu.

"I still haven't flown my kite!" said Mellie.

Lulu's parents looked at each other. Then out of the window.

"Mellie. . ." began Lulu's mother, but Mellie would not listen. Over the sand dunes she raced the family, and on to the wide sunny beach.

Not a breath of wind was blowing.

Not a breath of wind blew all that day. They tried the beach, and they tried the park, and they tried the high place on the cliffs where the castle stood. They discovered that no amount of running and tossing and adjusting and untangling will make a kite fly without any wind.

It was the last day of the holiday, and no kite flew. No dog from the sea saw it and came running. And nothing, not paddling, nor fair rides, nor even takeaway food from The Golden Lotus could make Lulu and Mellie happy.

The grown-ups were sad too. They had worked hard to make that kite fly, spent quite a lot of money, and driven through a great many potholes. They were unhappy about the dog from the sea as well. Secretly, they took it in turns to go and look for him. Lulu's father went for a long marathon-training run all through the sand dunes with dog biscuits in his pockets. Lulu's mother walked in the opposite direction with a bucket and a bottle of water. She stopped to talk with the people from the hot dog and ice cream stall, and with the lady at the bucket and spade shop.

Nobody had seen the dog from the sea.

In the evening, promises were made to Mellie. "We have to make an early start in the morning," Lulu's mother told her. "I'm sorry, Mellie, but I have to be at work at the hospital by lunchtime. . ."

Mellie nodded. Lulu's mother was a nurse, and both Lulu and Mellie understood that nurses have to be at work when they are expected.

"But the first windy day at home that

86

everyone is free we will all stop whatever
we're doing and rush to the park with
your kite! We promise! Don't we, Lulu?"

"Yes," said Lulu, "but. . ."

But it won't be the same, she nearly said.

"But what?" asked her mother.

"Nothing," said Lulu, because what
was the use of saying what everybody
knew.

The bare little cottage was tidied and
cleaned. Bags were packed. Sand drifts
were swept from the corners of floors.
Last of all, Lulu and Mellie and Lulu's
father smuggled the dustbin-lid rocks back
over the sand dunes. With the help of the
map they put them back on the beach in
their old locations.

"They look like they've never been
moved!" said Lulu's father.

That night the dustbin lid was left unguarded. Now that the dog from the sea had disappeared, he no longer seemed such an impossible idea to Lulu's parents.

"I expect Sam would have got used to him, after a while," they said, and they understood when Lulu put the leftover supper from The Golden Lotus in a bowl beside the dustbin, just in case.

They understood, too, when Mellie could not bear to pack her unflown kite. "Just let me keep it like it is until morning! Just to look at," she begged.

"All right, Mellie."

They even understood when Lulu insisted on keeping the bedroom window wide, wide open.

"But no getting out and camping by the dustbin!" said Lulu's father, astonishing Lulu, who had not even told Mellie of this most private idea. "Promise?"

"Promise," said Lulu, reluctantly.

"Go to sleep quickly then," said Lulu's parents, kissed them, and left.

Going to sleep quickly was not something that Lulu and Mellie usually managed. Usually they chatted for hours.

This time, however, they went to sleep quickly.

Mellie woke with a jump into a room
full of grey light.

It was dawn and it was cold, and
the air was full of a thin sound. At the
window the curtains were streaming like
flags into the room.

"Lulu! Lulu!" whispered Mellie. "The
wind is blowing!"

The wind *was* blowing, and Lulu's
watch said half past four in the morning.
They had hours and hours before the
grown-ups woke.

They did not pause for a moment.

Lulu put on her sandals.

Mellie picked up her kite.

First Lulu, then Mellie, climbed out of
the window.

The food from The Golden Lotus was
still untouched in the bowl by the bin.

 90

"But he'll see the kite," said Lulu, and followed Mellie across the patch of blue-green grass, into the sandy paths that wound through the sand dunes, and on to the empty beach.

A strong straight wind was blowing. A perfect flying wind. The kite, with its flock of bright seagulls, leapt into the sky.

From the moment the kite took off, Lulu and Mellie forgot everything but the need to hold on to it. It pulled on the strings like something alive. No flock of seagulls had ever soared higher.

The kite raced in front of the wind, and Lulu and Mellie raced along the beach behind, each clinging to a kite handle.

"Hold tight with both hands!" screamed Mellie, and it lifted them as they ran, so that they hardly felt their feet touch the sand. They felt nothing but the huge tug of the strings in their hands, and they saw nothing but sky.

For a long time, an unmeasurable amount of time, it was like running in an airy dream.

Then Lulu tripped and fell.

The kite-string handle flew out of her hand, and the kite, suddenly unbalanced, spun in a spiral,

poised in the air for a moment, and then
dived its whole flock of rainbow seagulls
head first into the sand dunes.

"Oh!" gasped Mellie, while Lulu picked
herself up. "My kite, my kite!" She started
running to where it had fallen.

Lulu followed more slowly, gathering
the kite strings and feeling her bumped
knees. She had time to look around
and see where they were. They were on
strange part of the beach, with unknown
sand dunes, far away from the little white
cottage.

Mellie was nowhere in sight.

Nothing Lulu recognized was anywhere
in sight.

Then, from somewhere high above,
Mellie screamed.

Lulu began to run.

In those unknown sand dunes the grey-
leaved, orange-berried bushes grew very
close and thorny. The sandy paths were
narrower, made for rabbits, not people.
The hollows were deep and unexpected.
The grasses grew over them and hid
them, so they opened suddenly, like traps.

"Lulu!" cried Mellie, and Lulu called back, "Where are you? Where are you?" and stumbled as she hurried.

It took a long time to find Mellie.

It was like trying to find someone in a maze.

But at last, there she was. Tumbled into a hollow, clutching her kite, and trying not to cry.

"I'm all right," she told Lulu, with her eyes screwed tight shut. "Only I've hurt my foot! I've hurt it awfully. . ." She gave a little sob. "I don't want to look. Is it bleeding?"

It was bleeding. Mellie had caught it on thorns, tripped, and fallen with it twisted beneath her. Already her ankle was puffy and swollen.

"Don't touch it!" she begged when Lulu bent to look, and then she did a very strange thing.

She yawned.

The earliness of the morning, the fright and the pain, were suddenly too much for Mellie. She switched them off.

She put her head on Lulu's lap and went to sleep.

For a long time Lulu sat thinking. She did not know what to do. She couldn't leave Mellie and go for help. It would take ages, and besides, she was not at all

sure, even with the kite strings to
follow, that she would ever find Mellie
again. And it was perfectly obvious that
Mellie could not walk back on such a
bad foot.

Nor could Lulu carry her.

We could shout for help, Lulu thought.
She tried a small shout. "Help! Help!"

The wind blew the words away and
lost them in the grasses.

I've got to think! she told herself fiercely,
and closed her eyes to help herself think
better.

A great brightness woke them both.

Blue and pink and gold. The morning
sky shone above their faces, edged with the
dark shadows on the long sand-dune grasses.

And high above, on the edge of the
hollow, they saw something else.

A long-legged, tatty, wind-blown
outline of a dog.

A dog who, from far away, had seen a
kite, and come running.

The dog from the sea looked down on
Lulu and Mellie, dark against the bright
sky, like an illustration from a fairy tale.

The dog from the sea stared at Lulu and Mellie in great surprise. He had not expected to find them when he had come running to investigate the kite. What were they doing, so far from their home? Where were their grown-ups, and what about Sam?

The dog from the sea tilted his head with its paper-bag ears one way and then the other, trying to understand.

They were talking. Hurriedly and worriedly.

"Go with him! Perhaps he'll take you back to the cottage!"

"What, and leave you here?"

"You could."

"You know I wouldn't!"

"I'm all right, Lulu, really I am. It hardly hurts if I keep still."

"What if you try and stand?"

"I don't know. Perhaps, if I had a bandage for my foot. In case it bleeds again."

A ribbon of kite tail made a sort of bandage, and then Lulu said, "Just try. I'll help. I'll balance you. . ."

"Ouch! OUCH! It's too tight! Don't pull! Let me go!"

Mellie fell back down into the sand, peeled off the kite tail, and whimpered a bit because her foot was now very painful indeed. The whimpering worried the dog. He backed away, whining.

"Good dog. It's all right," called Lulu soothingly, as she hugged poor Mellie, but she did not sound all right.

Neither did Mellie.

"What'll we do?" asked Mellie, between very damp hiccups. "How'll anyone ever know we are here?"

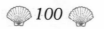 *100*

"They'll come and look for us," said Lulu bravely. "Soon as they get up and see we're not there. . ."

"How'll they know which way to look?"

"I don't know," admitted Lulu. "Perhaps they'll find our footprints. . ."

Lulu paused.

"They never will," said Mellie, and sobbed, a proper sob, and then another and another.

"Oh, don't cry!" begged Lulu, so miserably that the dog from the sea tumbled into the hollow to comfort them both. He licked salty fingers and rubbed his ragged head into their hands, not knowing what to do.

And then all at once, he knew exactly what to do.

Like a picture in his head the dog from

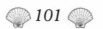

the sea saw the white cottage and the grown-ups belonging to his two unhappy friends.

They would have to be fetched.

He left Lulu and Mellie as suddenly as he had found them, leaping out of the hollow and vanishing amongst the sand dunes. He did not want to fetch the grown-ups. He did not want to go back to where the dogcatchers had been. For all he knew they might be there still.

But he could not think of anything else to do.

So he did it.

His long legs raced across the beach as fast as the cloud shadows raced across the sea. Mellie's kite-tail bandage, picked up at the last moment as he left, streamed behind him like a banner.

In minutes he was back at the cottage,
and there were the grown-ups, calling and
searching, up and down the sand dunes,
and in and out the house.

Sam saw him first.

"*WAR!*" barked Sam, but not very
fiercely. He was too tired to be fierce, he
had been up for ages with no breakfast,
trudging through the sandy paths, trying
to find the girls.

"*WAR!*" barked Sam, but he didn't
really mean it.

"WOOFF! WOOFF! WOOFF!" replied
the dog from the sea.

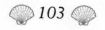

"Listen!" called the grown-ups, and they both came running.

"Look! Look! It's the dog from the sea!"

"Oh!" cried Lulu's mother and picked up the kite ribbon.

"He knows where they are!" Lulu's father exclaimed.

"WOOFF!" commanded the dog from the sea.

Anyone could tell what he wanted.

So Mellie and Lulu were rescued.

First came the dog from the sea.

Next came Lulu's father (very glad he had done so much training for when he might run a marathon).

Then Lulu's mother, keeping up very well, considering she had spent

the whole week reading book after book (although not *War and Peace*).

Last of all, Sam.

Sam did not run to the rescue; he walked.

Sam was only a little way along the journey when they all came back. He stopped when he saw the dog from the sea.

The dog from the sea stopped when he saw Sam.

But Lulu's father (who was carrying Mellie) said, "Don't be silly, you two!"

And Lulu's mother (who was carrying the kite) said, "You might as well make friends!"

And Lulu put them each on a kite-tail lead and led them back to the cottage, where Mellie's sprained foot was bathed and bandaged with an ice pack.

"There's no time for tellings off!" said Lulu's parents, as the bandaging took place. "But if there was. . ."

Luckily there wasn't. There was only time to fling the last things in the car, and somehow find an extra place on the back seat for Sam, because. . .

"You're never going off with that dog!" demanded the cottage owner, arriving just in time to see the dog from the sea being coaxed into the boot of the car.

"We are," said Mellie, smiling up at her. "Aren't you pleased?"

"Pleased! What are you thinking of? Isn't one dog enough?"

"The more the merrier," said Lulu's
mother.

"He's been wonderful," said Lulu's father.

"Well, good riddance, I say," said the
cottage owner, glaring. "But don't say I
didn't warn you! He's trouble, that dog! He's
a thief! He's a menace!"

"He's a hero," said
Lulu, and she
gave the dog
from the sea
one last hug
before she
climbed into
her seat
beside
Mellie

and Sam. "He's ours and we love him, and
we're taking him with us!"

★

Bump! went the car, through the first of the potholes, and then they were on the way home.